REDEMPTION MISTY MOUNTAIN

BONUS STORY

KINGRIDGE RANCH

ELSIE JAMES

Contact: Elsiejamesauthor.com

CHAPTER 1
ROSALIE

"HEY, *sugar. It's me, your favorite anonymous podcaster, here to give you the lowdown on who's doing what—or let's be real, who—in Sagebrush Creek. Grab your boots, 'cause it's time to get bitching and I've got more than enough sweet tea to spill today.*

You didn't hear it from me. But the word around Kingridge Ranch is there's a holy bun in the oven, and that little one just might be another in line for the Kingridge throne. Seems like those cowboys went from hard up to getting busy with half the town. Let's see if any of the brothers want to own up to it before I go sharing the name…

Meanwhile, over at Sow Much—"

"The podcast again?"

"Aaah—" I yank out my earbuds, nearly dropping my phone as I spin around to find my boss hovering in the doorway.

Ella laughs and crosses her arms. "Sorry, I didn't mean to freak you out. I can hear that shrill Texas accent from here."

I press a hand to my chest, willing my pulse to slow. "You scared the hell out of me! The *Boots and Bitching* is basically a community service at this point. If I'm about to live my cowboy ranch dreams, I need to know what kind of mess I'm walking into." I tilt my head. "Small-town Texas is *something else.* Shouldn't you be gone already? I thought I was the last one at the inn."

Ella shakes her head, amused. "You sound like Maggie. She's already blowing up my phone, telling me to get home before the storm hits. Even old Hank up the road has The Rusty Elk Tavern closed up already. But this place is—"

"Your baby, I know." I flash her a knowing look. "But trust me, I've got it handled. Cancellation notices went out and everything's locked up. I'm just making sure this place is spotless before I leave. The storm will pass and you'll come back without having to worry about anything."

Ella exhales and her expression softens "And *that's* why I'm going to miss you."

I shrug. "I'm pretty irreplaceable."

"That you are." She pulls on her coat, eyeing the door. "But I mean it. The roads are getting bad. Don't wait too long to head out."

I nod. "Yeah, yeah. I know better than to mess with Colorado weather."

Ella gives me a final look before stepping out into the cold.

As soon as the door clicks shut, I slip my earbuds back in and press play.

An hour later, I'm knee-deep in organization hell.

I've emptied every desk drawer, created a disaster zone, and promptly run out of momentum to clean it up. The podcast cuts off, and suddenly, the Hollow Tree Inn is too quiet.

A situation like this would normally creep me out. When you grow up with hellfire and brimstone, you learn a few things early. Ghosts? Real. The dark? Terrifying. And women who stick around in an empty inn with a snowstorm rolling in? They don't make it past the opening credits.

The silence settles deep in my bones and makes everything feel heavier. I glance around the empty lobby. The familiar creak of the floorboards under my feet is a reminder that this is my last shift. And somehow, that doesn't seem real.

When I came back to Misty Mountain, everything felt different. It was like stepping into an old life that didn't fit anymore. But Dad got sick. Mom had been gone for two years, and someone had to come back. There were only two options, Maisie or me.

The choice was obvious.

I was the one who had already broken free and shed the weight of our suffocating religious upbringing. In the span of five years, I'd gotten married and divorced to a man who stole my heart. We shined bright and burned out just as quickly. I'd lived on a cruise ship, backpacked through Europe, and of course, spent a summer on Kingridge Ranch in Texas. It's where I got my hands dirty in more ways than one. And where my obsession with *Boots and Bitching* started.

Maisie, on the other hand, had only just escaped.

She was just starting to imagine a life of her own. The older sister in me couldn't ask her to throw it all away. So, before she even knew what was happening, I packed my bags and came back to Colorado. What was supposed to be a temporary sacrifice stretched into a year and a half.

I won't lie. I resented it at first. Coming back felt like a life sentence with no end date. Like stepping into quicksand and watching the world move on without me. But then, Dad left faster than any of us expected. And in a town where nothing ever seems to change, my whole world shifted in an instant.

Now I watch the snow settle over the trees, the mountains standing quiet and unshaken. Two truths hit me in the silence. *This place will always feel like home. And there's nothing left for me here.*

But none of that matters now. In two weeks, everything changes again. I'll be back at Kingridge Ranch—this time with Maisie. She traded snowy mountains for open skies and professional athletes for ranchers, and maybe it's time I do the same. Maybe this time, I'll stay long enough to get a cat. Or at least a houseplant.

Buzz. Buzz.

The vibration in my pocket jolts me back to the present. I fish out my phone, glancing at the caller ID before pressing it to my ear. "Hey, I was just thinking about you out there with all those cowboys. How's ranch life treating you?"

Maisie's voice crackles with excitement. "Wild, Rosalie. You need to listen to the podcast. The Southern

Knights football team came through, and the Kingridge guys lost their minds."

I chuckle, already picturing the chaos. "I'm ready for the full recap. I've got a whole office to put back together."

As Maisie launches into a breathless retelling, I get to work, letting her words wrap around me like a story I'll be stepping into soon. Her laughter is contagious, and for the first time in a long time, I feel like things are falling into place.

Then I hear it. *Boom. Boom. Boom.* Three sharp knocks at the inn's front door make my stomach drop.

"Maisie, I have to call you back."

Boom. Boom.

Sliding my phone into my back pocket, I move cautiously toward the entrance. My pulse pounds in my ears. *A guest arriving late? Is it someone who can't see the obvious snowstorm rolling in? A delivery? Or something else entirely?* I scan the room for a weapon. *Fire poker? Kitchen knife? No, I'm being ridiculous. But then again… maybe I'm not.*

In a last-minute decision, I pick up a small, cast iron frying pan as I pass through the kitchen… Just in case I have to go Rapunzel on someone.

My pulse pounds against my ribs as I grasp the doorknob, the cold metal biting into my palm. One deep breath. Then another. I tell myself it's just some stranded traveler, someone who didn't check the weather report before heading up the mountain. Nothing more. I've got to get out of my own head. I twist the knob and pull.

The storm howls outside, a rush of icy air curling around my ankles, but it's nothing compared to the chill that races down my spine when I see who's standing on the other side. My jaw falls open.

It's Dawson. I blink a few times to make sure I'm not actually insane. But he's still here. Dawson is broader now. His shoulders are cut with strength and age. His presence is commanding even in silence. But there's no mistaking that it's him. It doesn't feel real. *How? Why? What the hell is he doing here?*

The ground shifts beneath my feet. Time stretches and snaps, twisting around me like a rubber band about to break. My body remembers him before my mind can even catch up—before it can summon the walls I spent years building brick by brick.

I see flashes of a life I've worked hard to forget. My first kiss. Our first reckless night together. The way he made me feel beautiful for the first time in my life. My heart slams in my chest, it's racing one million miles per minute.

Dawson's jaw is dusted with scruff that sharpens the angles that were always devastating. His deep-set eyes lock on mine. They gleam with that same streak of rebellion that once made me lose myself until there was no going back.

"Are you going to let me in?" His voice is a grumble. The snow clings to his dark hair and then melts against the heat of his skin and drips from the line of his heavy coat. "Or are you gonna hit me with that frying pan." He lets out a smug chuckle.

The sound of his laugh sends a flurry of rage

tingling through me. I take a half step away from the door, because what else can I do? He steps into the inn and just like that, the past shoves its way between us… bold and completely uninvited.

Infuriatingly, Dawson Stone is still the most handsome man in any room. Apparently, he's still the one who can steal my breath without trying. But he's also the man who made me believe in forever only to prove I was nothing more than an afterthought.

He's the man I begged to love me and the one I had no choice but to leave. He's the other half of the divorce that forced me into putting myself first and now he's standing in front of me and I think I might be sick.

I let out a heavy, frustrated sigh. His timing is unbelievable. I'm finally ready to move to a place where I can lay down roots. I'm at peace in my life, or at least I'm about to be… And now this. A thousand thoughts flicker through my mind, tangled and sharp. But only one finds its way past my lips as I shove the door closed.

"Perfect."

CHAPTER 2
DAWSON

THE SHOCK of seeing Rosalie slams into me like a lightning strike burning through every nerve ending. Having her right in front of me again is surreal.

Less than twenty-four hours. That's how long it's been since I finished my time in the Navy. I walked away from a life built on discipline, routine, and never staying in one place too long. I wasn't sure what to expect when I got back to Misty Mountain… But it sure as hell wasn't Rosalie standing here like a living, breathing reminder of everything I lost.

Rosalie—my Rosalie.

Only, she's not mine anymore.

I fucked that up. I let the most incredible part of my life slip through my fingers and I own it. But knowing that doesn't change the way she still fills the hollow space inside me, the part of me that's never felt whole since the day she walked away. She looks exactly like the last time I saw her, stunning, fierce, and impossible to ignore.

She feels like home in a way nothing else ever has. But from the look she's shooting me, I'd guess the feeling isn't exactly mutual.

Her hand settles on the curve of her full hip. It's a stance I know too damn well. She's stubborn, defensive, and bracing for impact. And yet, all I can think about is how many times I've had my hands there. I'm lost in memories of gripping her tight and holding on like she was the only solid thing in my world while I claimed her.

Her lips press into a full pout, and fuck if my body doesn't remember every damn thing about that mouth. How it felt against mine, how it whispered my name, how it wrapped around my pulsating length. I exhale sharply, forcing myself to look away, to think about anything else, but some things you don't forget. Some things stay carved into your bones no matter how much time passes.

And Rosalie? She's in every part of me.

"What are you doing here?" Her voice is sharp and clipped, but I don't miss the flicker of something beneath it.

I flash a slow grin, letting the moment stretch just to rile her up. "Nice to see you too, sweetheart. You really know how to welcome a hero home." I hang up my coat and lean casually against the mantle of the fireplace. "It's quiet here. Looks like we've got the place to ourselves."

My ex-wife exhales, a little exasperated, but not quite immune to me and I take that as a good sign. The corners of her mouth twitch, and I see her fighting it. Rosalie was never good at hiding things from me.

"This place is closed because of the snowstorm rolling in. All the reservations were canceled."

"Must've missed that memo," I say, unbothered. "Lucky for me, I guess. I don't have anywhere else to go. Not in this weather."

She mutters something under her breath and turns toward the check-in desk. "How long are you here?" Her tone is all business.

I hold her gaze. "I'm here forever. I'm done with the military."

I know it isn't the question she was asking, but I don't care. I want her attention and from the way her head snaps up, I've got it.

"Really?" For a split second, something flickers in those deep, knowing eyes of hers. Something warm.

"Yeah," I say, savoring the way she looks at me now. "Told you I wasn't in it for life. Checked my boxes, served my country, and now I'm free."

Her expression shifts in an instant, soft curiosity hardening into something colder. "Yeah. Being in things for life isn't exactly your strong suit."

The hit lands square in my chest. "Ouch," I say, dragging a hand through my hair. "That's fair." I hold up my hands in surrender. "I'll go get settled in. My reservation is in room one. And just so I know… what room are you staying in?"

She crosses her arms over her chest and it's one of my favorite sights in the world if I'm being honest. The round swell of her full tits press up and there isn't much I wouldn't do for the chance to bury my face in them one more time. I check her left hand. No ring.

"I'm not a guest," she says flatly. "I work here. Or I did. This is my last shift. I'm leaving right now before the roads ice over."

Something sharp and unwelcome twists in my gut. "It isn't a good idea. They're already slick. Are you still driving that tiny Toyota, because without chains, you really shouldn't?"

She shakes her head like I don't have any right to be protective of her, and maybe I don't. But I can't help it.

"I am leaving, and not just the inn, Dawson. I'm done with Misty Mountain, too." Her voice is steady, and I don't miss the sharp edge beneath it. "I'm heading into a whole new life, far away from here. So you can have this place all to yourself."

The words spill out of her thick with the weight of everything left unsaid between us. It's not just a statement… it's a warning, a clear line drawn in the sand. But for right or wrong, I make the decision right there to ignore it.

"I'm sorry to hear that." *And I hope I can change your mind.*

She must read the determination on my face because Rosalie walks behind the front desk. She retrieves a key for room one with a huff and slides it across the counter toward me. Then she stomps away without another word.

CHAPTER 3
DAWSON

I HAUL my suitcases in one by one and brush off the fallen snow as I enter the inn. The wheels drag over the threshold with a dull thud and the snowflakes dissolve into wet spots. I make it up the staircase to the first room and unlock the door to my new home… for now.

The inn smells like cedar and memories I haven't had time to face yet. As I unpack, I keep one ear tuned to the hallway. My muscles are tight with anticipation. If Rosalie thinks she can slip out without talking to me, she's dead wrong. I'm not ready to let her go. There's too much left unsaid and I need to apologize. I need to know she's okay. More than that, I need her to know that I never stopped loving her.

I yank the heavy curtains open and my pulse is a steady drum in my ears. It's an idyllic view. The snowy mountains create a backdrop for the endless quiet of the forest that stretches out in front of me. It's breathtaking even under the heavy weight of my thoughts.

Snow falls in thick, lazy sheets, blanketing the world

in white. It should feel peaceful, but it doesn't. Not without her. How did I manage to screw this up so completely?

My parents didn't teach me much; except how to survive when the odds are stacked against you. *When you're poor, the world doesn't care.* That was the lesson drilled into me early. *No one's coming to save you. You want out? You claw your own way up.*

The military was my way out. The only way. But it came at a cost. One I didn't understand until it was too late. At work, they loved me because I never said no. Tricky deployment? Yes. Stay late? Yes. Arrive early? Yes. Give more, be more, sacrifice more? Always yes. There was no cost too big to write my ticket for a secure future.

Now I've got more money than I ever imagined. But no Rosalie. So what the fuck was the point?

At the time, I never thought I was choosing my job over my wife. But hindsight has a way of cutting straight to the truth. I did. I chose wrong in a million tiny ways until I finally lost her. I exhale, watching the snow morph into sleet. The wind rattles against the glass. I glance toward the driveway. Her car is still there… Good.

I'm not done with her yet.

Being this close to her again has supercharged every nerve in my body. I forgot what she does to me and the way my body reacts to her on auto-pilot. My skin burns and my muscles are tight with the kind of tension that only one thing can ease. I need relief.

I need to take the edge off before I lose my goddamn

mind. All the blood in me rushes south, it's thick and demanding. My cock strains painfully against my zipper. I curse under my breath as I lay back on the bed, dragging a hand over my stomach before reaching down to unbutton my jeans.

My mind doesn't have to wander far. Memories of her flood in, taking hold, making me harder. I can't take it. I slip my hand beneath the waistband of my boxers, a groan ripping from my throat as I wrap my fingers around my cock.

I picture Rosalie's wide, innocent eyes looking up at me years ago, her pupils blown with heat. The way her lips parted when I kissed her. The quiet gasp she always made when I deepened it. The feel of her curves pressed against me, soft and warm, the way she used to melt into me like she belonged there.

My tip grows slippery. I can almost hear her breathless little whimper that I pulled from her every time I ran my tongue down her neck. I stroke myself slowly, savoring the fantasy. My grip tightens as I picture her beneath me. Her thighs trembling, her nails digging into my shoulders, and her lips forming my name in a breathless plea.

Fuck. I'm so hard it's almost painful, my hips lift off the mattress as the need for release builds. It's sharp and relentless. Rosalie is all I can think about. The way she felt. The way she *sounded*. The way she came undone in my arms, gasping my name like I was the only man in the world.

My jaw clenches as pleasure coils tight, ready to

snap. I bite back her name, the taste of her memory thick on my tongue as I finally give in.

Everything goes white-hot, heat crashing through me in a dizzying wave. And then—nothing. For a split second, I'm weightless, untethered, lost in the bliss of release.

Until a sound outside my window yanks me back to reality.

My eyes snap open, my breath is still ragged and my body thrums… and then I see her. My stomach drops. I yank the comforter over me so fast I nearly roll off the bed, my pulse hammering. She's still staring, wide-eyed, her mouth slightly open, a flicker of something unreadable in her expression.

Rosalie? What. The. Fuck.

She's right there. My jaw falls open, and her name tumbles from my lips for a whole new reason. "Rosalie?"

We lock eyes and she blinks. I blink. Time slows to a crawl as my brain catches up to what's happening. First, the sheer horror hits me. *Did she see me? Oh God, did she see me?* But then, another realization slams into me like a truck…*How the fuck am I making eye contact with her when I'm on the second floor?*

I zip up my pants with lightning speed, my heart still hammering in my chest, and fly to the window. But my absolute *horror* only deepens when I realize Rosalie isn't even looking at me.

She's balanced precariously on a damn ladder. A *ladder* that she's wedged into the bed of my truck… in the ice storm. Even worse, she's leaning out too far.

She's reaching toward the massive tree beside my window.

My pulse spikes as my eyes snap to the tree, following her line of sight. And that's when I see it. A tiny orange cat. *No fucking way.*

"Of course. Of course, she's out here in a snow-storm, halfway to breaking her neck, for a goddamn cat." I grumble to myself until her name escapes my chest in a bark. "Rosalie! What the *hell* are you doing?" I fumble with the window, but it doesn't unlock.

I pull on my boots and coat then take the stairs two at a time.

This woman is going to kill me. Or herself. Or both.

CHAPTER 4
ROSALIE

"COME ON, it's okay. You are okay. I'm right here." I stretch out a hand toward the tiny, shivering ball of fluff clinging to the tree branch. "You can't be more than a few weeks old, and it's freezing out here. Let's get you inside."

"ROSALIEEEEEE, GET DOWN!" Dawson's voice explodes through the quiet forest, slicing through the eerie stillness of the storm.

I flinch, gripping the ladder tighter. "Shut up, you're scaring him," I snap over my shoulder. "The Kitten Distribution System has finally come for me!"

"And you're scaring me!" He sounds closer now, his boots crunching over ice-coated ground. "That is *a cat*, Rosalie. You do realize they *climb trees*, right? They're born knowing how to do it."

"Thank you for that," I mutter, inching higher. "I *know* she can climb, but she's *not*. She's scared, freezing, and I'm not leaving her."

"Yeah? Well, you *should*, because in case you haven't

noticed, *there's a damn ice storm happening*." His voice sharpens. "Get down. Now. Or I'm coming up."

I ignore him and focus on the kitten. The metal rungs under my boots are slick with ice, and I have to move carefully. One wrong step and I'll be the one needing rescuing. But I'm not stopping. Not now.

"Easy, baby," I whisper to the kitten, holding out my hand. The kitten takes a half step toward me and I lunge toward her. "I've got you."

I catch his front paws and pull him into my arms, tucking him into my jacket. He hisses and paws at me with furious determination. But I don't hold it against him. The poor thing can't be any older than five months. I breathe a sigh of relief.

I take a cautious step down the ladder and then. *Chomp.* Pain explodes in my cheek. The little monster bites me. I let out a yelp and flinch. That's all it takes. The rung beneath my foot shifts. My stomach drops. My grip on the ladder wobbles.

Oh. *Crap.*

"Dammit," Dawson growls, his voice laced with panic.

It's the last thing I hear before I'm *falling*—not a graceful, cinematic fall, but a chaotic, limb-flailing *cascade* down the ladder, hitting each rung like a human pinball. It does nothing to calm the kitten who is currently fighting his way out of my shirt and digging his tiny paws into me.

I brace myself for the cold, hard, *painful* impact against the ice. But it never comes. Instead, I crash into something *solid* and *warm*.

With a grunt, Dawson stumbles back. His arms lock around me and steady me despite the force of my fall. It takes a second for my brain to catch up. It's one long, disoriented heartbeat where the world tilts and everything feels upside down. By the time the spinning slows enough for me to process what just happened, I realize—

He's *carrying* me.

Through the threshold of the inn.

Like I weigh nothing. Like he hasn't done this exact thing before.

"Oh my—"

"Get the damn cat out of your jacket and *sit down,*" Dawson barks, his voice sharp, edged with frustration.

But there's something softer in it too… Is it a concern? Worry? I blink, still slightly dazed as my feet hit the hardwood floor. The second I let go, the orange menace explodes from my jacket like he's been shot out of a cannon. He hisses as he vanishes beneath the overstuffed chair in the corner. *What a big baby.*

"Are you hurt?" Dawson's voice shifts, the bite is gone and replaced by something gentler. "I need you to sit down so I can see what that demon did to you."

I do as I'm told. Not because he ordered me to, but because my legs still feel like Jell-O. I sink onto the couch in the lobby as Dawson disappears into the kitchen. A moment later, he's back, pressing a warm mug of tea into my hands.

I stare at it, still catching up. Then he reaches for the zipper of my jacket and I freeze.

His fingers graze the fabric, tugging it down with

quiet efficiency. The second the cold air hits my skin, goosebumps ripple across my arms like a traitorous confession. It's like my body remembers things I'm trying really, really hard to forget.

I force myself to focus anywhere but on him—on the warmth of the tea in my hands, the slight tremble in my fingers. But then I glance down, and my stomach tightens. Blood. A smattering of red has seeped through the fabric of my white shirt, spreading in tiny, clawed patterns.

"Oh, sweetheart." Dawson's voice is a low, gritted growl.

It's rough, edged with something that nearly *undoes* me.

"Look what he did to you." His fingers brush the hem of my shirt. "Take it off."

My breath catches, but I snap out of it fast. "What? *No*."

"Jesus, you are so damn stubborn." Dawson exhales sharply, his jaw tightening. "It's not like I haven't seen it before. I need to clean up the bites. The last thing we need is for them to get infected while we're *trapped* out here."

I cross my arms. "I'm not *trapped*. I'm heading home as soon as I can coax him out and get him in the car with me."

Dawson's eyes widen, a flash of incredulous anger sparking behind them. "The hell you are, no." His voice drops an octave, firm, unyielding. "No one in their right mind is driving down that mountain right now, and I'm not about to stand by and let you try. Especially not with a demon cat in tow. You're here until the storm passes. With me. Like it or not."

The storm howls outside, rattling the windows as if to hammer Dawson's point home. I clench my jaw, refusing to back down. But then something about the way he looks at me makes my knees go weak. There's frustration in his eyes, sure, but underneath that, there's something quieter.

I exhale sharply and sink back into the couch. Now that the adrenaline is wearing off, the sting of the wounds on my chest settles in, sharp and insistent. Besides, it's been a long time since anyone wanted to take care of me. "Fine."

I peel my shirt over my head, wincing slightly, and catch the way Dawson's eyes darken. Not just with concern. There's an *ache* there. It's subtle but unmistakable. To his credit, he tries to keep it together.

He presses a hot towel to the swell of my chest, his fingers brushing against my skin as he cleans the bites. His touch is careful and deliberate. The heat from the towel is nothing compared to the warmth pooling in my stomach.

We don't say much while he works his way across the top of my bra. But something about the silence feels almost *too* natural. Like this isn't the first time. Like it wouldn't take much to slip back into something dangerously familiar.

It'd be so easy to fall back in love with this man.

"There you go." He clears his throat, breaking the spell. "I'll grab you a clean shirt from my bag and light a fire on this thing." He stands and puts a hand on the fireplace's mantel.

"A fire would be nice, but I've got clothes," I murmur, forcing my voice to stay even. "I have my gym bag in my car."

I start to push up. But before I can so much as lift myself off the couch, Dawson's hand is on my shoulder, firm and steady, pressing me back down.

"I'll get it," he says, voice low, leaving no room for argument. A slow smirk tugs at the corner of his mouth. "Don't want to risk you seeing some kind of bear or maybe a cougar you want to save."

Just like that, the spell is broken. "Don't be an asshole."

CHAPTER 5
DAWSON

TWO HOURS LATER, I've made the most of my unexpected alone time in the inn's kitchen. The fridge is stocked like someone was planning to ride out the apocalypse here.

The shelves are packed with fresh produce, expensive cheeses, and even a bottle of white wine with a label so fancy I have to squint at it. I'm not much of a wine guy, but I know enough to guess Rosalie picked it out. She's always had good taste in wine… and in bras.

Tracing the lines of her cleavage on the couch was the best kind of torture. It took two cold showers to get over the tingles it sent whipping across my body. If I don't get it out of my head, I'm going to need another.

I shake off the thought and focus on the pan in front of me, tossing in another handful of freshly grated parmesan. The upside to trying to win back my ex-wife is that I already know all the tricks in the book. I haven't seen much of her in the last two hours, but if there's anything that'll lure her out of her room, it's pasta.

Back when we were married, I never cooked for her. Not once. I was too busy, too distracted, and too convinced other things mattered more. But after I lost her, I made it my mission and learned how to do it right.

Tonight I needed something rich and indulgent. My goal was to figure out what she'd close her eyes for on the first bite. The answer was right in front of me… garlic, butter, and parmesan.

The pasta's done, the chicken's nearly seared to perfection, and the air is thick with the scent. It's a damn masterpiece. I let it simmer for just a minute longer to give the sauce time to do its thing.

In the meantime, I scoop a few tiny bites of chicken into a dish for my reluctant dinner companion. With a sigh, I carry it into the lobby. "Come on, cat, order's up."

Silence… Figures.

I scan the room, spotting the little devil's glowing eyes from beneath the couch. I crouch down, then decide to fully commit. Stretching out on my stomach, I rest my chin on my forearm and lock eyes with him. His pupils narrow into slits, his ears flatten.

I smirk. "What, you don't like hot chicken on a cold day? You wanted to starve up there on that icy branch?"

He responds with a low, rattling hiss. I throw one right back, a quiet, mocking sound through my teeth. "You're lucky I'm feeding you at all. I haven't forgotten what you did to my girl. Eat your damn chicken."

A pause.

Then, like the spiteful little bastard he is, his tiny paws shoot forward. Before I can react, sharp teeth sink right into the top of my hand.

"Son of a—" I yank back with a yelp, barely avoiding smacking my head on the coffee table. "You're a real asshole, you know that?"

By the time I recover, he's already snatched the chicken and retreated into the shadows, probably smug as hell about it. I glare at the darkness under the couch, flexing my hand.

A soft crunch echoes back at me and I turn to see Rosalie and get to my feet. She's got all my attention. She stands in the doorway, bathed in the soft glow of the inn's lighting. She's a vision wrapped in tight, black spandex that clings to every inch of her curves. The woman is all thick thighs and soft hips. Her tank top hugs just enough to make my brain short-circuit.

"Are you fighting with the kitty?" She arches a brow in my direction.

"He started it."

Her lips twitch, but she doesn't smile. And damn, I want to be the guy that makes her.

"Come on, I made you dinner."

I push open the kitchen door and let my hand settle against the small of her back as she steps inside. It's just a light, barely there touch, but through the thin fabric of her workout top, the warmth of her skin seeps into my palm. I force myself to ignore it.

"It smells incredible in here," she says, glancing around. "But since when do you cook?"

I flash her a grin. "I'm a changed man."

Her gaze sweeps over the kitchen as she takes in the details. The flickering candlelight, the low hum of music playing from my phone, and the stove alive with bubbling pans.

I pull out a chair for her at the kitchen countertop, and that gets me what I've been waiting for… a smile.

It's soft with just a hint of amusement, but it's there. And it's real. Damn if it doesn't hit me like a fist to the chest. I clear my throat and plate the pasta like I know what I'm doing.

One hour and a half bottle of wine later, we're talking like old times. The kind of easy, effortless conversation that makes it feel like no time has passed at all. Rosalie giggles when I admit to all the hours I've spent glued to the cooking channel, and shakes her head in disbelief when I tell her it's become my secret passion.

In the candlelight, she's even more breathtaking than I remember. She's the same Rosalie with a massive heart and the kind of charm that makes you want to take care of her. Only now she's stronger and more sure of herself. It's sexy as hell.

"Okay, tell me again… What's the podcast called?"

"It's Boots and Bitching!" Her eyes light up. "It's this anonymous, robot voice in Sagebrush Creek. She… or maybe he, I guess, literally knows everything about everyone in the town. It mainly focuses on the brothers of Kingridge Ranch, but that's because they're practically royalty out there. Maisie says—"

"Ugh." I groan, cutting her off with mock disappointment. "Are you still on the cowboy thing? Remember the way you swooned over an old man when I took you to Garth Brooks?"

Her jaw drops in exaggerated offense. "Excuse me? He's Garth. Brooks. Swooning is required."

I shake my head like it's a damn tragedy. "Ranchers have nothing on this." I flex my bicep, giving it a solid pat for effect.

And just like that, I get my reward—full-bodied laughter, the kind that lights up her whole face and makes her eyes crinkle at the corners.

Damn. I missed this.

"Since we are getting to know each other again, let me ask… What exactly were you doing when I glanced in your window earlier?" She erupts into a fit of giggles and I bury my face in my hands.

"Ah, shit… Leave it to you to call me out," I laugh.

This girl is too much.

From there I let her talk about her plans for a new life in Texas with her sister. A hollow ache thrums in my chest. Memories flood back to me in waves, but they're all anchored in regret.

This could have been my life. Cooking dinner for the most beautiful woman I've ever known and falling asleep tangled up with her.

Rosalie pauses and takes a sip from her glass. "Can I ask a serious question? Why couldn't you have done this while we were married?" She chews on the corner of her bottom lip.

"Well, that's simple. It's because I was an idiot. I thought we needed a full-on ranch to have the quiet life you wanted. I thought I was getting us there, but instead, I lost you. The loss of a lifetime."

She turns to face me. Her eyes are glassy and I don't know if it's from the wine or the conversation. But I reach out and put my hand over hers. She doesn't pull away.

"I'm sorry, Rosalie."

I hesitate just long enough for my pulse to hammer against my ribs. Then I close the space between us. And when our mouths meet, it's earth-shattering.

It's a slow burn that ignites the second our lips touch and crawl across me. Heat, memory, longing—it all crashes over me at once. Her breath hitches, and I tighten my grip, pulling her closer, like maybe if I hold on tight enough, neither of us will break this time.

Our tongues tangle, the kiss deepening, turning desperate. A low sound escapes me as I bury my hands in the back of her hair, twisting my fingers into the silky strands.

I plant a kiss on the spot behind her ear because I haven't forgotten the way it makes her come unglued. For a moment, it works. She melts against me, her body molding to mine, her breath warm and ragged.

Then—just like that—she pulls away. The warmth of her vanishes, leaving behind nothing but cold air and the taste of her still lingering on my lips.

"I can't," she whispers, her voice raw. "I'm not ready to break my own heart again when I leave for the ranch. I already know how this ends."

She looks at me then, her dark eyes shimmering with something that cuts straight through me. Regret.

Sadness. The kind of certainty that makes my chest tighten.

"It doesn't have to end at all, not this time."

"No, I chose you once," she murmurs. "But I have to choose myself this time."

The words land like a punch, knocking the breath from my lungs. I should say something. Fight for this. For her.

But right now, all I can do is watch her step back—watch her slip through my fingers all over again.

CHAPTER 6
ROSALIE

I RETREAT to my room and sink onto the bed. My pulse is still erratic from that kiss. If I'd stayed in that kitchen a second longer, I would've unraveled completely. I've come too far and fought too hard to reclaim myself to let it go now.

I can't throw it all away for a kiss even if my lips still tingle with the memory of his. My head and heart pull at each other in an impossible tug-of-war with Dawson at the center. I've been here before, but that doesn't make it any easier.

In the end, I decide to turn my brain off and my Kindle on. A book boyfriend is clearly the safest choice for the night. A half hour passes and I'm lost in the pages… Until everything goes black.

I use my almost dead phone as a flashlight and creep to my door, opening it just a crack. Darkness swallows the entire inn and presses in on all sides of me. My chest tightens, a flicker of panic sparking in my veins.

"A freaking power outage, are you kidding me right now?"

How long is it going to be before this room becomes a refrigerator?

I climb back in bed and try to keep my cool. *I'm an adult. This isn't a big deal. It's just a little… uncomfortable.* The storm rages outside of my window and everything is illuminated in the white light of the moon. I don't love it, but I can't get in my own head right now either.

Tap. Tap.

"Sweetheart, are you okay?" Dawson's voice cuts through the black. It's steady and warm, wrapping around me like a blanket.

I exhale slowly. "Of course. Why?"

The door opens and his footsteps pad toward me. Each one is deliberate and unhurried. "Being places like this all alone used to creep you out and you never liked the dark."

"I never liked being left in it," I murmur.

He knows me too well.

I feel him before I see him. Dawson's presence is so grounding and familiar that I could cry. He reaches for me in the darkness, and without thinking, I reach back. He sits on the edge of my bed and a heavy silence stretches between us. His fingers brush a strand of hair away from my face.

"If I could go back and do it all differently, I would."

My throat tightens. "We can't go back."

"I know, I know." His voice is a whisper.

His arms slip around me, and Dawson pulls me into his warmth. His heartbeat thrums steadily against my cheek. And despite everything, the past, the wounds, and the walls I've built… I let him hold me.

Wrapped in his arms there's a dangerous sense of rightness that whips through me. His embrace is strong and familiar. He tightens his hold on me like he's afraid I'll slip away. And maybe he's right to be.

I should pull back. I should remind myself why I left and why I'm so desperate to build a life without him in it. I try to fight it. I imagine ranchers and a life on a farm beside my sister. But it's no use, my body melts into his.

His woodsy scent seeps into my senses. His fingers trace lazy circles on my back, his touch featherlight, reverent. My breath hitches when he presses his lips to my temple, lingering for just a beat too long. My heart hasn't forgotten the way our bodies fit together.

"Dawson, we can't go back, but we have tonight. It won't change anything but I've missed you and…" I turn to face him.

He shifts back just enough for me to see his face. He doesn't say anything, but I see the response in his eyes. I feel it in the way his fingers ghost over my hip, in the way his breath mingles with mine.

The air is thick between us. It's charged and waiting. My pulse drums in my ears as his hand slides up my arm, tracing the curve of my shoulder, the column of my neck.

I shouldn't do this… but I do.

I turn my face to his touch. My lips brush the heel of his palm. His breath shudders out, and the sound makes something deep in my stomach twist. His forehead presses to mine, and for a long, silent moment, we just breathe the same air. The past and the present collapse into each other, and suddenly, there's no space between us. I close my eyes and plant my mouth back on his.

"Rosalie." My name on his lips is laced with hesitation. It's half a whisper and half a prayer.

"I'm sure," I whisper because I am.

His lips find mine all over again. It's slow at first like he's memorizing me. But then I'm kissing him back in a frenzy of desire. My fingers grip the front of his shirt, pulling him closer and needing more.

The storm rages outside, wind howling through the trees. But here, wrapped in Dawson's arms, there's only heat.

His kisses blaze a trail down my neck, causing me to shiver as his lips brush my skin. Dawson's hands grip my shoulders and press me into the pillow with an intensity that ignites every nerve. I am consumed by the sensation.

He plants soft, sweet kisses across the scratches on my chest. Then his mouth is urgent, and ravenous as he descends further. Dawson's hair is soft and slightly damp as it grazes against my chest. I exhale, releasing the weight of the past while his mouth sears a path across my skin, leaving a burning trail that tingles long after.

Dawson presses a hand to my inner thigh and I let my legs fall open for him. He runs his tongue down the length of my glistening slit and I feel the sensation shoot through me.

I gasp, clutching his head with trembling fingers,

pulling him closer with a desperate need, craving him impossibly nearer. Shockwaves surge through me, yet he is relentless and his pace unyielding. He takes his time working me until my body wracks with trembles and I'm thrusting my hips up to meet him. I'm desperate for more friction and he's happy to give it to me.

When he kneels in front of me, I grasp his firm length between my fingers and find he's throbbing with need for me. Dawson slides inside, filling me in a single thrust. My walls collapse along his length as he rocks into me.

The electric hum of the energy between us shuts out the cold from the raging snowstorm outside and right now, I hope it never ends. I give myself to him completely.

I am stretched taut, caught between the comforting warmth of his presence and the exquisite agony of his touch. The whole world fades around us as the sensations peak and he drives me toward the edge.

When I let go, my voice breaks the silence like a sudden clap of thunder. The sound is his name pouring out of my mouth like it never left. It's like Dawson is the only man who has ever known how to love me. My body trembles with waves of pleasure that pull him under with me. Hot streams fill me and I take all of him until the last drop.

The snow doesn't let up for nearly five days… and neither do we.

Dawson and I keep it light. We don't worry about the impending reality and instead, we take the honeymoon we never had. We make up for lost time in ways neither of us could have imagined. He's taken to wearing nothing at all, and I've taken to shamelessly appreciating the view.

We make love on every surface of the inn. We get lost entirely in each other and in the heat that never seems to fade. The power flickers in and out, but I barely notice. It's hard to care when I'm trapped beneath Dawson.

Even the cat has warmed up to our little slice of heaven. I've taken to calling him Garth, though Dawson refuses in the name of hating cowboys, so he still calls him cat.

Garth's not exactly a snuggler, but he makes his presence known—occasionally slinking past us with a judgmental flick of his tail. I even caught him napping on Dawson's back once, like he, too, had surrendered to the warmth of this unexpected truce.

But today, the sun is out. With it comes reality, crashing in through the sound of my phone ringing.

Maisie.

When I answer, her voice bursts through the line. It's bright and full of excitement. She rambles about the podcast and how she can't wait for me to get to Kingridge Ranch. She's lined up a job for me at the Buck and Whinny Horse Stables on the property and secured an apartment with a spare bedroom. It's everything I've been working toward. The fresh start I promised myself.

I hang up and reality looms over me. What are Dawson's long-term plans? Does he have any? Did he ever achieve the security that was so important to him? Or is this break from the military just a chance to start over on another dream where everything and everyone around him will be pushed to the side?

Life in Texas is waiting for me and it's everything I wanted. Everything I planned for... So why doesn't it feel quite as thrilling anymore?

CHAPTER 7
DAWSON

I WAKE up to the devastating glare of the sun cutting through the curtains, an uninvited reminder that the world outside still exists. Yesterday, day five of heaven with Rosalie, the ice had started to melt. But I made my case for staying and it stretched the fantasy a little longer.

Today, I already know that won't work.

This place will shift back into the Hollow Tree Inn in no time. I half expect to see tires crunching up the path at any minute. This week has been a taste of a life that could have been with Rosalie and it's more than I ever imagined. But the spell is breaking and I'm not ready. Not now. Not ever.

With a sigh, I pull on clothes for the first time in days, the fabric stiff and foreign against my skin. I don't love it. But the odds of someone who isn't Rosalie walking through those doors are getting higher by the second.

I scan the room. It's too quiet. Too empty.

Where is she? A flurry of movement followed by a flip of an orange tail catches my eye. "Cat, have you seen her?"

Cat, my reluctant, asshole of a roommate lifts his head from his nest on the armchair but offers no answers. Rosalie's side of the bed is cold and that's what really gets me moving.

I find her behind the front desk, hunched over the computer with her fingers tight on the mouse. Her forehead is lined with worry and her lips are pressed in a way that makes my chest go tight. The shift is here. I can feel it. The way the air between us isn't charged with heat anymore, but something heavier can't be a good sign. I don't like what's coming. Not one damn bit.

"Hey, sweetheart."

"Hi."

I circle the desk, slipping my arms around her from behind. I press a kiss against the side of her neck. But I already know something is off. She feels stiff and distant… I don't like it.

I continue, "What are you up to this morning?"

Rosalie exhales, her hands still on the keyboard. My stomach clenches because I already know the answer before she says it

"The only thing left to do, I'm getting ready to go back to my real life."

The words cut straight through me and leave a hollow feeling in my chest. But I'm not going to let her walk away that easily. I'm going to stop this before it starts. I spin her chair so she's facing me. Then plant both hands on her shoulders in an effort to anchor us into place.

"So don't," I say, firm but gentle. "Don't leave. Let's do this the right way this time. Me and you against the world."

She shakes her head. Her eyes fill with something that twists in my gut like a blade. "Come on, Dawson. Don't make this any harder than it already is... You don't even have a plan," she says, voice steadier than I'd like. "I looked. Your reservation here is for three months." She gestures toward the computer like it's the final nail in the coffin. "What am I supposed to do? Move in with you here at the inn?"

"What?" My head jerks back. "You're sticking with your plan and just taking off? You have no—"

"No… right?" Her voice rises, heat flaring in her eyes. "I have no right to question the plans of the man who put me in second place to his plans for the entirety of our marriage?"

I flinch. "That isn't at all what I was going to say, but clearly you aren't done." I fold my arms across my chest.

"We tried this before, Dawson. It didn't work and I told you from the moment you arrived that I was on my way out of this life." She presses a hand to her chest, her breathing sharp. "I never cared about money. All I wanted was you. But you wanted your career and your plan. You wanted the dream more than you wanted me.

And for what? To end up living in a hotel?" She lets out a shaky laugh like she's disgusted with herself for even entertaining this. "Come on. Don't put me through this again. I have to choose myself this time... You can see that, can't you?"

My pulse pounds in my ears and I try to control my fury. "You have no idea what the hell you're talking about." My voice is low and rough. "I know I messed things up back then, but give me some credit here. I've grown. I'm not the same person, and I would hope you can see that after the last few days."

She swallows hard, but her eyes are already retreating. I can all but see her pulling back from me and it's breaking my heart.

"My sister has a job waiting for me," she says quietly like she already knows this is the final blow. "I'm going to start my life on Kingridge Ranch."

I bark out a bitter laugh. "The fucking ranch again. Yeah." My jaw locks, hands fisting at my sides. "If it's that important, you better go then."

She lingers for half a second—just long enough for hope to crawl up my throat like a damn fool. I should've never let my guard down. Should've known better. There isn't a single thing I can say that will change her mind. I'm going to have to show her. And that's not something I can do at a moment's notice.

She exhales, shifting on her feet. I want her to say something... anything.

"Dawson, will you make sure Garth—"

Anything but that.

"I'll take care of the damn cat." My voice is tight, clipped.

Her lips part like she might respond, but instead, she just nods. "Thanks."

And then she turns and walks away. This time, I'm the one being left behind. And damn, does it sting. I've got to get to work.

CHAPTER 8
ROSALIE

SIX WEEKS *Later*

The door to our apartment creaks open, and Maisie steps inside. Her cheeks are flushed and her boots kick up bits of dirt onto the mat. Her shirt and jeans are covered in mud.

"I have an hour before I have to be back up at the stables and that horse got me good. He's going to take some work... I'm going to hop in the shower."

"The perks of living in the same place you work... It's all yours."

I've been sick for a full week. But honestly, it doesn't feel all that different from the other five weeks I've spent here at Kingridge Ranch. Except for the nausea, the dull throb of lifelessness I'm experiencing has been consistent. I'm more existing than living and the emptiness is painful.

The whiplash from spending five magical days with Dawson on a snow-covered mountaintop to crashing in a cramped apartment with my sister under the endless expanse of Big Sky Country is almost too much to handle. Before, when I thought I'd never see Dawson again, it was easier to shove the past into a locked box and pretend I'd moved on.

But knowing he's back, knowing he loves me, and having fresh memories of the way his body feels on top of mine is like taking a punch to the gut I never saw coming. Every breath feels too heavy, every thought circles back to him, and no matter how hard I try to settle into this new life, my heart refuses to let go.

When Maisie gets back, her eyes are wild with excitement. "I'm sorry you still aren't feeling well… But I have to tell you what just happened, you aren't going to believe this." She refills her water bottle and grins over at me. "The Southern Knights football team is coming back to the ranch, and all the Kingridge guys are losing their damn minds. I was trying to finish my training session with the new mare when total chaos broke out—" She stops mid-sentence, narrowing her eyes at me. "Are you okay?"

"Yeah, I'm fine. Tell me more." I try, but it comes out flat, and she reads me like a book.

"Yeah, right. This isn't a sickness." Maisie flops onto the couch beside me, crossing her arms. "This is like, what? Day one million of you moping around? What happened to "I'm going to get to the ranch and start my cowgirl era?"

I sigh, tucking my knees under the blanket. "I guess the cowgirl in me likes a book and a quiet evening at home more than a bunch of ranchers plotting revenge on a professional football team. Also, that stupid ass rooster chases me every time I walk to the stables."

"Choke." She raises an eyebrow at me.

"What are you talking about?" I roll my eyes.

"Choke the Chicken… He's more of a guard dog in a rooster's body. I've come to like him. All you have to do is stand your ground. It's a trick I learned. You should try it, you can't befriend him." Maisie lets out a chuckle and I want to be there with her, but I just can't.

I sigh, "I'm the problem, it isn't the ranch. In fact, I'm starting to think I'm the problem in most areas of my life." *Especially when it comes to love.*

Maisie squints at me, her eyes run across my face like she's searching for a missing clue. "Yeah… see, that kind of thinking is what I call insane behavior." She gestures at me. "I've been on this train of thought since you got here. Here are my theories. One—you hate it here. Two—it isn't as fun as the last time you visited. Three—you've suddenly developed a deep-seated hatred for burly ranchers."

I snort. "We can't all be spending quality time in the Udder Satisfaction Milk Barn with a certain handsome Kingridge brother." I glance at her, smirking. "Tell me, what was the expiration date on that V-card of yours?"

Maisie's face ignites like a bonfire. It's cruel but effective. We were raised in what my parents called 'the church'—but what I've since come to think of as a full-on cult. She's still shaking off some of the guilt they baked into us, so I know exactly where to hit.

"Would you shut up? The window is open and you know how this place is, that will spread like wildfire. Besides I—" she starts, flustered.

I hold up a hand. "Relax. I'm not actually asking for details. And the gossip around here is how I found out in the first place. When I heard that a new horse trainer might be shacking up inside of the Udder Satisfaction Milk Barn with a Kingridge brother, there were only two options and I knew it wasn't me."

Maisie exhales hard and bites back a laugh. "Okay, okay we can circle back to that… I may have *something* to share. But right now we're on you, not me."

I laugh, but the moment fades as quickly as it came. "I don't hate it here," I say finally, my voice softer now. "It's just… I ran into Dawson before I left, and to be honest, he's all I can think about."

Her jaw drops. "Dawson-Dawson… Like, the Dawson? Here? Dawson Stone is in Texas?"

"No, back in Misty Mountain before I left…" And just like that, the whole story spills out of me. One detail at a time. Even the steamy parts.

I don't mean to, but once I start it feels good to bring someone into my world. I tell Maisie how right it felt to be in his arms again and about the way I hoped the snow would never melt. I tell her how for a moment, it felt like coming home.

And I tell her the hard parts too. I tell her how the illusion shattered with the sunlight. I talk through his lack of a plan and the way I know he'll put everything on the back burner as soon as he comes up with a new goal. Maisie listens in stunned silence. Her lips part slightly, her forehead creases, and her expression stays unreadable.

When I stop rambling, a long silence stretches between us. I feel lighter for the first time since the moment I left Dawson at the Hollow Tree Inn. But talking through it makes it real too and I miss him with the kind of deep ache I haven't felt in years.

"No wonder," she finally says. "It makes so much sense now. I kept thinking maybe you'd end up with one of the Kingridge guys, but it never felt right." She shakes her head. "Of course, they can't compete… Dawson's always been your person. You can't just replace that. Not even with a cowboy in very tight jeans."

I let out a weak laugh.

"So what happened after you left?" she asks. "You moved here and stopped talking to him? Again?"

I nod. "Pretty much. This time it was more my fault than his. He texted me each night on my drive to make sure I'd arrived safely and then once I got settled in. It was non-stop and I had to tell him to stop."

Maisie groans, covering her face with her hands. "No, you didn't… You really didn't. And he listened?"

"He said that if he couldn't tell me who he is now, he'd show me. That was two weeks ago."

She groans even louder. "Ugh, I already hate myself for what I'm about to say because living with you is literally all I've wanted since you left home. But… you've got to go back. You have to go back to Misty Mountain and give him a chance."

My stomach twists. "And what if I end up right back

where I was after the divorce? He's got no money, no security. He's going to chase some dream, and I'll be on the backburner all over again."

Maisie tilts her head, watching me closely. "But what if it's different this time? What if he's actually showing you that he's grown into the man you always believed he could be?" She leans forward, grabbing my hands. "I'll be here. Kingridge Ranch is it for me. You can live here anytime. Except right now." She gestures around. "You're just... existing here right now. And that's not you. You haven't even made it onto a single episode of the Boots and Bitching Podcast. That's embarrassing."

I bark out a laugh despite myself. "I know you're right. In my gut, I believe him. I think I'm scared."

Maisie squeezes my hands. "Then do it scared."

I swallow and my throat is tight. She's right. I know she's right.

"Yeah, I will."

When she leaves, the emotions I've been keeping at bay bubble up all at once.

Dawson is the reason my heart has felt like it's been stuck in a pressure cooker for six weeks straight. He's the reason I can't settle, no matter how hard I try. He's the only man I've ever loved. It's never been over for me and it still isn't.

I throw back the blanket and stand, my muscles protesting after three days of being curled up on the couch. I grab a pair of jeans from my closet. But when I catch my reflection in the mirror, something stops me.

My breasts are tender. There's a nausea that I can't

seem to shake. When was my last period anyway? The thoughts don't even have time to seep through me before I reach my conclusion. "Oh shit… I'm pregnant."

"You're pregnant?!" Maisie's voice comes from the other side of my door loud and shrill.

CHAPTER 9
DAWSON

"EXCUSE YOU, BRO."

A walking brick wall of a man clips my shoulder as I step back into the dark corner booth of The Rusty Elk Tavern. The guy reeks of alcohol and bad decisions. His bloodshot eyes barely register me before he staggers toward the bar.

I roll my eyes. *I knew I didn't want to be here.*

"Yeah," I mutter, my voice low and edged with irritation as I take a sip off the top of my beer.

My grip tightens around the bottle and my jaw clenches as I shove past him. He doesn't realize how lucky he is that I've got bigger things on my mind. Because ever since Rosalie left, I've been looking for a reason to unload on someone.

But right now isn't the time. It's almost sunrise and I haven't seen my bed yet... Not that it's anything new.

The last few weeks have been a blur of long hours and restless nights. Every spare second has been spent trying to fix what I broke. Because getting Rosalie back is the only thing that matters. Nothing else registers, not even sleep or food. They're all just distractions. I don't even know what I'm still running on. Fumes, maybe. Stubbornness, definitely.

The only thing new is the fact that I'm standing in a tavern in a half-assed attempt to unwind. And I've got Ella to thank for that.

Ever since the Hollow Tree Inn came back to life, Ella's been buzzing around me like an over-caffeinated hornet. Yes, she owns the place which also means she's technically my landlord. But that doesn't explain why she's made a damn hobby out of throwing unsolicited advice my way like it's her life's calling.

When Ella first told me about these monthly gatherings, I laughed in her face. I told her it sounded like a bunch of washed-up heroes hitting the bottle harder than they should. She didn't argue. Instead she just slipped a flyer under my door. And then another. By the third one, I had to admit the description fit me a little too well.

Most of the time, I let it roll off me. But tonight she wore me down and the next thing I knew, I was standing in the doorway of the Elk for Beer and Darts Night. I was already regretting my life choices as she shoved a beer in my hand and wandered off to find her wife.

Now here I am. Several drinks deep, no closer to sleep, and still just as wired as when I walked in. Rosalie's face is burned into the back of my mind, a loop I can't shut off. And no amount of beer or forced small talk is gonna change that.

I thought coming here would be a massive distraction. But once I stepped through the doors, I realized I was wrong. This place isn't bad.

The Rusty Elk is your typical small-town bar with wood-paneled walls, scuffed floors, and the faint scent of fried food permanently soaked into the air. It's the kind of place where the beer is always cold and the music is a little too loud for my taste. The regulars come as much for the gossip as anything else and their names are practically carved into the barstools.

Hank, the owner, is an ex-Marine. He's older but still built like a tank and with a voice that could make a grown man snap to attention. He throws these monthly gatherings for all of us ex-military saps who can't get our shit together… his words, not mine. But he's not wrong.

I've been out of the military for over a month now, and nothing feels settled. It's like I walked out of one warzone and straight into another. Only this time, there's no orders… only chaos. And Rosalie's at the center of it.

She's gone from my world again and it's left a void in me I'm not sure I'll ever fill. That's exactly why letting her go isn't an option. My mission is clear. I've got to get her back but it's taking longer than I planned and every extra minute is killing me.

The night's been a decent change of pace with more than one familiar face in the crowd. Old voices swap war stories and the occasional burst of laughter cuts through the low hum of conversation. I downed an entire pint before I was ready to make eye contact with anyone. But the waitstaff didn't miss a beat. I'm pretty sure they've seen this routine before.

Groups of locals gather to trade gossip over rounds of whiskey. A few women throw smiles my way, but they don't land. I keep my head down.

By the second drink, I threw some darts with an old Army buddy, Finn. He's a solid guy, always was. He tends to be on the grumpy side but I didn't hate catching up if I'm being honest. Turns out, he's been putting the pieces of his life together, or at least trying.

He's doing okay for himself now… He's figuring out how to make civilian life work. It made a pang of jealousy stab through me. It made me wish I could settle into my next chapter. Like this is all just another deployment to get through.

But our chat made it clear that I'm still stuck between past and present. It's like my boots are caught in the mud and no matter how hard I pull, I can't get loose. Four drinks in, mid-game with Finn, it really hit me. *Maybe there's something wrong with me. Maybe I'm the one screwing this up, making it harder than it has to be.*

Then I ran into Griff.

The guy looked like he was being tortured just standing here. His shoulders were tight and his eyes scanned the room like he'd rather be anywhere else. And that felt right to me. That made sense.

He and I didn't need words. Just a quick head nod of understanding. A silent acknowledgment that neither of us had this whole retirement thing figured out. That we weren't the only ones struggling to make sense of life outside the uniform.

Now I'm more drunk than sober. I'm slouched alone at the back table under a dimly lit bulb. My thoughts are the only company I've got and it's how I prefer it right now. I'm lost in a pool of self pity and an insatiable drive to finish the project I've started.

There's got to be a way to move faster. Hire more people. Get more done.

A hand on my shoulder startles me back to reality. I look up to see Ella reappear beside me. I don't appreciate the distraction.

"Yeah?" I blink up at her.

"Hey, it's late. We're getting out of here," she says, nodding toward the exit just as her wife, Maggie, appears beside her.

Just what I need, a front row seat to a happily married couple.

"Great. See you tomorrow," I mutter, settling back into my chair.

Ella lets out an exasperated sigh. "No, you jackass, *we* are leaving. As in, you and us. We're taking you back to the inn for the night. You can pine away over Rosalie from the comfort of your room instead of stinking up this bar."

I huff out a breath, but I don't have any fight left in me. Not for this. "Fine, but I'm finishing this beer first."

Ella plants a hand on her hip, one eyebrow arched like she's already ten steps ahead of me. I take a slow, deliberate sip, dragging it out just to be the jackass she's pegged me for.

Then Garth fucking Brooks bellows through the speakers. The sound is loud and twangy. It cuts through the bar like a goddamn assault on my eardrums. And that gets me to my feet.

"I hate this song."

"Great, I'll be sure to play it in the car," Ella laughs.

CHAPTER 10
DAWSON

STEPPING into room one doesn't hold the same luster as it did with Rosalie by my side. I'm in a drunken state of blurriness as I start my nighttime routine. Then I catch my reflection in the bathroom mirror and damn, it's a rough sight. I've got dark circles, blotchy skin… I look like hell.

The beer finally does its job and after a quick shower, sleep is all I can think about. *I only need a few hours and then I'll head out to the jobsite and be right back to it.* Stepping out of the shower, I pull open the door to my room, my towel slung around my waist. I pull open the door to Room One and scan for a flash of orange fur, but there's no sign of him.

"Cat," I bellow down the hall. "Get up here. I'm back. If you're sleeping in here, you've got two minutes before I close this door."

All I hear in response is silence. No fuzzy tail. No begrudging shuffle of paws and truthfully… It's fine by me. Cat and I have come to an understanding. We're somewhere between reluctant roommates and friends. But I won't lie, I've taken to liking the way he curls up on my back at night.

Cat isn't impressed with my new schedule and he sure as hell doesn't understand what it's going to take to bring Rosalie back into our lives. So I lay down without him. I fall asleep the moment my head hits the pillow. I close my eyes and dream of all the ways I'm going to show Rosalie something she can't ignore when this is done.

Boom. Boom. Boom.

I ignore the light tapping I've been hearing for the last five minutes. But three sharp, urgent knocks at my door have me bolting upright. I don't know how much time has passed, but I know I'm not ready to get up.

"Hold on." My words are a bark as I slip a pair of pajama pants on.

The person standing on the other side of that door better have a damn good reason for all that noise. When I rip the door open, I'm taken aback. It's Ella… again.

She's probably following up about last night. It's annoying, but the thought of her and Maggie taking care to drive me home softens me just a bit. How the hell does she look so perky and awake?

"Hey, thanks for getting me back last night."

Ella raises an eyebrow at me. "I'm happy you went. That was a good decision."

"Oh come on, like I had a choice? You only slipped a

flyer under my door, sent one up with my breakfast tray, and told me that you put a personal phone call in with Hank. But yeah, I think it was a good thing. Might as well make some connections now that I'm back. I'd rather they not be so early if I'm telling the truth." I widen my eyes.

Ella laughs. "Apologies for the wakeup call." Her hands are tucked into the pockets of her hoodie and her smile fades. Concern etches into the lines on her face. "I know you just got in a few hours ago, but…" She hesitates. "There's something I think you should know."

"Okay." *I doubt it.* My jaw tightens. Nothing short of an emergency is getting my mind off Rosalie.

"It's about Rosalie."

My pulse jumps and all of a sudden I'm wide awake. "You have my attention."

"There's a podcast, I'm not sure if Rosalie told you about it. It's some small town gossip thing that gets recorded in Sagebrush Creek… You know, that ranching town." she says.

She woke me up for a fucking cowboy podcast?

"Yeah, I'm aware of the podcast, thanks. To be honest with you, I don't give a shit about the podcast or anything else in the town besides Rosalie. If that's all, I'm going to—" I step back inside, but Ella puts a hand on my door and holds it open.

"If you could get out of your own way, you might give a shit about the latest episode." She turns with a shake of her head and my door closes behind her.

What the actual fuck? I know that she and Rosalie were close, but I couldn't imagine that she'd be spending her time listening to some podcast from halfway across the country. I shake my head and make a pot of coffee. Then I find the damn podcast on my phone and press play on the latest episode.

'Hey, y'all. Sagebrush Creek, I've got some extra sweet tea for you today. Y'all pull up a chair. It's your favorite secret podcaster, back with another boots-on-the-ground update. You know the drill—I've got my ear to the ground and my fingers on the pulse of this town's messiest secrets. So y'all pull up a chair and pour something with a little kick because this one is bigger than the Texas sky.'

The voice is a high-pitched, back-of-the-throat Texas twang transmitted through some kind of voice changer and I already regret my decision. This is going to be ten minutes of my life I'll never get back. But if it has to do with Rosalie, I'll bite. I'm not getting any news updates about her life in any other way. I sip my coffee and try to stomach the sound as it continues.

'And when I say big, I mean… baby big.

That's right, folks. Rumor has it there's a new bun in the oven right here in Sagebrush Creek. The only problem is. I don't have all the details yet and I'm not one to gossip.

Here's what I do know. There's a little cowboy (or cowgirl) on the way over at Kingridge Ranch. And the two names floating around? None other than those new horse training sisters… Rosalie and Maisie.

Now, I don't have confirmation which of these lovely ladies is about to become a mama, but let's just say the evidence is piling up. Rosalie's been keeping a low profile ever since she showed up from Misty Mountain Colorado. Then there's Maisie… Let's just say she's been avoiding the bourbon at The Velvet Spur. My money is on the older one because some of us were here during her first rodeo at the ranch and it's gonna take more than a few years to make those memories fade into the sunset.

I know y'all are yawning because this podcast is for the locals and those ladies ain't from here... But the daddy sure might be.

This baby might make another heir to the ranching throne. Could it be one of the Kingridge brothers? Because let's be honest—those boys have been dodging commitment like a bull in a rodeo arena for years, but lately, we've been seeing them get roped in. Or maybe, just maybe, someone else in town is about to get the surprise of a lifetime.

I've asked around and mums the word... for now. But think about it sugar, there ain't too many cowboys in this town smooth enough to knock those holy boots off the Reagan sisters. If the rumors are true, this could be the biggest scandal to hit that ranch since Pa Kingridge's third divorce. If I were a betting woman, I'd keep my eyes on the Kingridge Ranch. After all, nothing says family legacy like an unexpected heir.

One thing's for sure, Sagebrush Creek... this little secret won't stay hidden for long. And you know I'll be the first to spill the tea when it all comes out. I'll be watching. And trust me, so will the rest of this town.

Until next time, darlings. This is your bitch with boots on the ground, signing off.'

I sit in stunned silence as the episode ends.

The words echo in my head, overlapping, unraveling, until the pieces finally snap into place. I reach back for memories of my former sister-in-law Maisie and I immediately know, it isn't her. From what I remember, she's all in on purity culture and the rest of that churchy bullshit.

That leaves… Rosalie. My heart rate ticks up and my chest tightens. Rosalie is pregnant.

My pulse slams against my ribs as I flip open my phone, swiping through the calendar. How many weeks has it been? I count backward, my fingers moving faster, my brain refusing to keep up.

Is it possible? Can it be true? And if it is— Is it even mine?

That last thought has me leaping up and reaching for my car keys. I've got to get out to that damn ranch whether I'm ready or not.

CHAPTER 11
ROSALIE

I PULL the last of my clothing out of my closet and shove it into the same moving box I pulled it out of just a few weeks ago. It's been two days since a dozen at-home pregnancy tests confirmed what my body already knew. I'm pregnant.

I've spent two days riding an emotional rollercoaster that took me from disbelief through denial and fear, past acceptance, and now, somehow, to excitement. It's a strange thing, carrying both terror and joy in the same breath. But here I am, clutching onto the one certainty that refuses to be drowned out by doubt.

I'm having Dawson's baby… and apparently, he's going to be the last person to find out.

Thank god the man has an aversion to all things cowboy because thanks to our open windows, I've officially made the podcast. I have to tell Dawson as soon as possible, but this isn't the kind of thing you can do over the phone.

The man deserves to hear the life-altering news in

person. Besides, there's something about the thought of him as a father that lights something deep inside me. It's like a flickering ember of hope waiting to catch fire.

The timing of this pregnancy was a shock, but Dawson and I creating a life together is a picture that I've painted in my mind more times than I'd ever admit. Every time I close my eyes I see Dawson cradling a tiny, dark-haired baby with his easy smile and steady hands. The man was born to be a dad. He's protective, patient, and good.

Of course, the fact that we aren't exactly speaking at the moment isn't ideal. And there's the fact that the last time we were in the same room the air between us was thick with unsaid things and with old wounds that never quite healed.

But still, somehow, I think he'll be happy. I might be delusional, but it's the truth.

Tap. Tap. Tap.

"How's the packing going?" Maisie steps into my nearly empty room.

"It's pretty easy when you don't start with much to begin with."

She lets out a laugh. "Make sure you don't slip my new headphones into that bag… They're missing."

I chuckle at her accusation. "Did you check the washing machine? I swear I heard something clicking around in there."

"Ugh, this is the third pair… I'm losing one per month. Do you want anything? I'm going to make a quick lunch before my next training session. You know what, never mind, I need to feed my niece or nephew.

I'm making you something, I'll leave it on the countertop."

I shake my head. "Thank you."

My heart aches. Maisie has been covering my shifts at the stables, stepping in without hesitation, like she always does. The thought of leaving her behind in Texas when we've only just started to rebuild our relationship makes my heart lurch. After everything we endured growing up—the loneliness, the weight of surviving in a house that never felt like home—I thought we'd finally carved out something solid, something lasting.

Now that we're free from the shadows of our childhood, I'd hoped to make her a permanent fixture in my life. Not just stolen weekends and phone calls squeezed between work. Real, everyday life.

And now, with a baby on the way, that pull is even stronger. My child deserves an aunt like Maisie—someone fierce and loving, someone who understands what it means to fight for happiness.

But I can't do this without Dawson.

So I'm packing my bags for Misty Mountain. And tomorrow, at first light, I'm heading straight back to the man who still holds every piece of my heart—whether he wants them or not.

Two hours later, there's nothing left to do but wait… and waiting has never been my strong suit.

I've eaten the lunch Maisie left me, packed every last thing I might need, and scrubbed the apartment down even though it didn't need it. Then I wrote Maisie a note thanking her for always being on my side.

For the first time in days, I feel lighter. Clearer.

With my bags by the door and nothing to tether me here anymore, I step outside to soak in these last few moments of life on this ranch. The afternoon sun bathes everything in gold, stretching long, dappled shadows across the fields. The air smells like warm hay and horses, and a part of me aches at the thought of trading this in for snow.

I thought this was it for me. I thought I'd find my place here and set up a future. But my place is with Dawson and he is zero percent rancher and all Misty Mountain Man.

In the distance, a group of farmhands lingers near the farm stand. Their heads angle toward one another, then whip toward me in unison… And that's my cue to cut a path through the field.

I'd rather not answer any questions for them to dissect. Instead, I give them a wave then veer off course, cutting past Thrusty the goat's pen. My chances are better with a notoriously horny goat than with a group of ranch hands itching for fresh drama.

I'm almost clear when the distant sound of shouting pulls me up short. The air shifts, tension rippling through the quiet. My gaze snaps toward the open stretch of land, my feet moving before my brain catches up.

There's a man yelling. And I know my mind must be playing tricks on me… because that voice sounds like Dawson.

As I close the distance, the scene comes into focus. Three of the Kingridge brothers stand outside one of the main houses, their voices loud and taunting. Their postures loose but together they form a mountain of unmistakably aggressive men. They're not just shouting… they're heckling.

It's a sight I've come to expect after living here. I bite back a laugh. This time their target is a lone man in a cowboy hat. It isn't even close to a fair fight. The dude is standing stiff-backed in the middle of it all.

To make matters worse, Choke, the infamous attack chicken, is fully committed to the ambush too. He's flapping and swooping at the poor guy's ankles with ruthless precision. Anyone who stumbles onto Kingridge land without an invitation is either leaving with a bruised ego or a solid pecking wound… sometimes both. That poor fool doesn't stand a chance.

Bits of the conversation drift to me on the breeze in sharp snippets of words… *Did old Mayor Randolph send you? He's just a chicken, walk away from him. That's what I thought. That hat ain't even yours. Your name doesn't start with an E, does it?*

But I get closer and things shift into focus and—

"What the hell?"

I blink to make sure I'm not seeing things, but it's true. The man under interrogation is Dawson… My Dawson. And he's wearing a cowboy hat of all things.

"Hey, hey!" I shout and wave my arms at the mob as I pick up the pace. All eyes turn to me. "Stop it, I know him."

"You know him?" Alexander Kingridge yells back toward me and there's an edge to his voice.

"Rosalie, thank god. These fucking weirdos and

their damn rooster are holding me hostage. We would never treat people like this on the mountain. What the fuck, man?"

"Oh, come on now, that ain't true. You aren't stuck. Told you we'd let you pass as soon as you can rope a calf, show us that you've earned that hat." Callum Kingridge lets out a whoop.

"No, just toss a horseshoe into the pit. That's all it'll take to put this to rest," another brother adds with a laugh. "Or how about we arm wrestle? You win, I call off my big bad chicken."

Dawson grits his teeth, ignoring the guys completely and turning to me. "Is it true?" His voice quiets the group.

My eyes widen and I freeze. *Is he asking about the pregnancy? Does he already know about the baby? No, he can't be.* "I uh—"

"Yes, tell us. Is it true that you bought that hat at the gift shop on the way in?" Bowen Kingridge asks, biting back a laugh and the guys erupt into laughter like a bunch of real assholes.

I push through them and stand beside Dawson. "That's enough—" I start to shout, but the door to the house flies open with a creak.

A curvy blonde woman steps out onto the porch with a hand on her hip. "Y'all get out of here and take the damn rooster with you. Leave them to it. I swear y'all are a bunch of children sometimes." She turns to face Dawson and me and her face softens. "Excuse them."

I don't know who she is, but she seems to speak

Kingridge. The guys disperse around us in an instant and Alexander steps into the house, tail between his legs. *That must be Cassidy, the mayor's ex-wife I've heard so much about. I'm sure glad she showed up.*

When the chaos finally settles, I don't think… I just move.

I grab Dawson's hand, threading my fingers through his, and tug him off the path. I lead him into the privacy of the tall golden stalks of the wheat field. I don't want an audience, all I want is him.

The world narrows to just the two of us. All I hear is the whisper of the wind and the steady drum of my own heartbeat in my ears. I can't believe he's here. I can't believe that after everything, we've landed in the same place at the same time and that there is a life growing inside of me… one we made together.

My nerves overtake me. What if he doesn't want anything to do with this baby? What if I'm wrong? What if this sends him cascading into another plan where he'll never have time for a child?

I open my mouth to speak and my voice wavers between laughter and disbelief. "Dawson, I… Well for starters, I never imagined seeing you on a farm. And in that hat, it's a really nice touch. I'm so flustered, I can't believe this is real. What are you even doing here?"

He ignores my rambling. His chest is rising and falling fast, his breath uneven. We lock eyes and it sends a wave of calm rushing through me. I love this man. I can trust him with this.

When Dawson finally speaks, his voice is rough,

thick with something I've never quite heard from him before. "Is it true? Are you…?"

His hand tightens around mine, his pulse pounding so hard I swear I can feel it thrum beneath my own skin.

I swallow back the anxiety clawing at my throat. "It's true."

The air shifts. Something breaks open between us.

Dawson's eyes shine, filling so fast with tears that stun me. He doesn't even try to fight it. He lets the tears spill freely and his face is raw with emotion.

"It's true," he whispers like he needs to hear it again, to believe it with his whole being. "Holy shit, it's true."

His hand drops, sliding gently over my belly. His touch is tentative at first, then firm and more sure. His fingers brush my skin and something inside me unravels.

Tears sweep across my cheeks. "Dawson, I love you so much. Thank you for coming here. I don't know how you found out but I was on my way to you. I've packed up my whole life—"

"I love you, Rosalie. Nothing was going to keep me from getting to you. I never dreamed I'd be lucky enough to have two chances with you," he says, voice breaking. "But I'm all in. You and this baby are the best things that ever happened to me."

"I don't know where we'll live or how—"

"I've got us covered." A smile tugs at the corner of his mouth. "Let me get this damn hat off and show you what I've been working on."

CHAPTER 12
DAWSON

I GET Rosalie in the truck and grip the wheel like it's the only thing keeping me tethered. She chatters about the pregnancy. She tells me that she's counting down the days until she can drink coffee again without feeling like a traitor to her own body. Then she talks about the last six weeks on the godforsaken ranch. I hate the thought of my girl with a bunch of asshole cowboys, but I keep my mouth shut.

She's mine again. And my world feels right.

I answer at least fifty questions about Cat who Rosalie still insists on calling Garth. Meanwhile, my pulse pounds in my ears, drowning out everything except the sound of her beside me. I take in the cadence of her voice. The way she huffs every time I dodge one of her more pointed inquiries and the way she's here… With me.

I'll never take her for granted again.

I keep my focus because I can't get off this ranch fast enough. Not because I want to leave Kingridge, though

I sure as hell do. But because I need to get her to where we're going. It isn't finished yet, not even close, but I hope it's enough to prove to her that I've changed.

I'm not the man who let her slip away before.

I punch the address into my phone and my stomach tightens. It's my first time visiting this place too, and the thought twists something sharp in my chest. I barely glance at the screen before pulling onto the road.

Rosalie is beside me, close enough for me to reach out and trace my fingers over the back of her hand. I do and the quiet satisfaction settles in my bones. I know she thinks she's gearing up for a drive back to Misty Mountain, but I don't want to ruin the surprise. When I ease onto the shoulder fifteen minutes later, she looks at me with wide eyes.

"What? What's wrong? Do you want me to drive for a while?" Rosalie turns, brows knitting together.

I let out a slow breath. The silence between us thickens. It's weighted with something unspoken. *This is it.*

"No," I say, gripping the wheel. "We're pretty much there. This is where we were heading." I hit the brakes, then make a left, guiding us onto a dirt road. The truck bounces as I search for the mile markers.

"What?" Rosalie's jaw falls open, but I keep my eyes on the path ahead.

Dust billows in the rearview mirror, thick and golden in the late afternoon sun. The land stretches out before us, open, raw, and flat as hell. Then finally, I see it. My heart slams against my ribs as I kill the engine.

Adrenaline pushes me forward before I can say a word. I shove open the door, rounding the truck before

Rosalie can start firing questions my way. I pull her door open and gesture outward.

"Welcome to Plot 78." I put my arm up. "Look at the mountain."

She turns to me, her brow furrowed, eyes flashing with skepticism.

"Dawson, sweetheart," she says, voice slow and measured. "Have you completely lost your mind?"

I huff out a laugh, shaking my head. "I think I might have, yeah."

We walk the outline of our six-acre property, one step at a time. We are hand in hand and it feels right. The land is quiet and untouched. There aren't any towering pines like back in Misty Mountain. But there are plenty of sturdy oaks with their sprawling branches stretching toward the sky. Low brush and wild grasses blanket the ground and somewhere in the distance, a deer lifts its head at the sound of our footsteps, ears twitching before it vanishes into the tree line.

Rosalie's fingers tighten around mine as we move, her gaze sweeping over the land, taking in every detail. I watch her carefully, searching for any sign of what she's thinking, but she's unreadable—just quiet, observant.

I clear my throat, steadying myself. "I knew you needed to be close to your sister, so I drew a boundary around that damned ranch and searched for a place to build. Somewhere that could be ours."

She looks up at me, curiosity flickering in her eyes.

"But the reason I picked this spot," I say, giving her

hand a light squeeze, "is because of that. We have our own mountain."

I nod toward the rise in the center of the property. It's not much—just a hill by any reasonable standard—but here, in the middle of all this open land, it stands tall.

Rosalie lets out a glassy-eyed giggle, tilting her head as she studies it. "You're calling that a mountain?"

I grin. "Sure. In Colorado, we'd call it a hill," I admit. "But from what I can tell, it might be the highest point in Texas."

She shakes her head, but she's smiling now, laughter still in her eyes. It makes something inside me loosen, just a little.

I take a breath and keep going. "I've got a team back in Misty Mountain working on every piece of our dream home. We've been at it around the clock. We're building it there and assembling it here. Now that we've got a new family member on the way, we'll have to make a few adjustments, but that's fine. We'll figure it out. All those years in the military weren't for nothing. We are secure. I've invested and saved for a life I didn't know I'd get another chance at. But I promise you, I can take care of us from here on out… Forever."

Rosalie's lips part slightly, her breath catching. Tears cascade down her cheeks. "Dawson," is all she says. But she leans into me and I wrap my arms around her.

I kiss the top of her head. "I stayed at the inn for three months so they could start this project. Of course, I didn't expect to have them put it together in Texas, but I also didn't expect you to walk back into my life either." I give her a small, lopsided smile. "So I'm counting that as a win."

Her eyes well with tears, her chest rising on an unsteady inhale.

"Dawson," she whispers, her voice thick with emotion. "I'm sorry I doubted you for a single minute. You are incredible. I can't believe you—this—any of it." She presses a trembling hand to her mouth, shaking her head slightly before looking at me with nothing but love. "It's always been you."

And just like that, I know. She sees it. She feels it. She's home in my arms.

EPILOGUE: ROSALIE

A few weeks later

Early March brings rare Texas snowflakes with it. They are delicate and fleeting as they drift lazily from the sky. They melt the second they touch the golden grasses. They're another reminder that we aren't in Colorado anymore.

This is not Misty Mountain with the heavy, endless snowfalls that once blanketed my world. This is different, but still thrilling even though I could have never planned on it. Snowfall brought Dawson back into my life. Snowfall outside of the Hollow Tree Inn gave us a backdrop for our wedding. Now it's snowing again, but this time, I'm already in his arms, exactly where I belong.

I adjust the thick knit blanket wrapped around my shoulders and lean against the wide windowsill, cradling a warm mug of cinnamon tea in my hands. The home Dawson built for us is stunning. It's all open windows and exposed beams mixed with cozy fabrics.

It stands strong, nestled against the rise of our very own Texas mountain. The hill is Dawson's pride and joy. Truthfully, it's become mine too. I love it because it's ours. Every time I think of all the layers of effort that Dawson put into building this place it brings tears to my eyes. This place was made with love and stubborn determination, and I still can't believe it's real.

We're settled… truly settled now. And after a lifetime of searching, I didn't think I'd ever be able to say that.

Strong arms wrap around my waist from behind, pulling me against the solid heat of my husband. I let myself sink into him, into the comfort of being his again.

His lips graze the side of my neck, the lazy rasp of his voice sending a shiver down my spine. "Still trying to convince yourself that it's real snow?"

"If it's frozen and falling from the sky, it counts," I argue, taking another sip of tea.

Dawson huffs out a low chuckle, his hand smoothing over the curve of my belly. As if on cue, our baby kicks, a firm little reminder that life is moving forward in the best possible way.

I grin. "I think he agrees with me."

"He inherited my impeccable sense of logic," Dawson muses. "Won't catch this guy climbing a tree in an ice storm to save a cat."

I roll my eyes and Cat lets out an offended meow from the corner of the couch.

"So not cowboy logic then? Because I was thinking… if we're really settling in Texas, we should embrace it." I turn my face up to him with a wicked smile. "What do you think about naming him something strong? Rugged. Like Maverick. Or Colt. Or, I don't know… Tex. A real rancher name."

Dawson groans, his head tilting back in sheer agony. "Rosalie. When I tell you there is not a chance in hell—"

Laughter bubbles out of me, but I loop my arms around his neck and let my fingers play with the hair at his nape. "Fine. But I reserve the right to call you Daddy Dawson."

His hands tighten at my waist. His expression darkens, his lips just a breath from mine. "Say that again, sweetheart, and we'll be working on baby number two before this one even gets here."

Heat whips down my spine and anticipation curls low in my stomach. I bite my lip, ready to test that theory—

Boom. Boom. Boom. A sharp knock at the front door shatters the moment.

Dawson groans, dropping his forehead to mine. "You invited your sister, didn't you?"

"She doesn't need an invitation." I grin and pull away, already hurrying toward the door. "Maisie!"

I yank it open to find her bundled in her thick coat, her cheeks flushed pink from the cold. But it's not just the chill in the air giving her that glow. There's something softer in her face, something hesitant and full of quiet excitement. Her hand rests protectively over her stomach.

The sight makes my heart squeeze just like it has

from the moment I found out. "Come in, come in. We're just getting ready to start a fire."

She gives me a knowing smile and steps over the threshold. Then she turns to Dawson with a shrug. "Looks like the cousins wanted a playdate."

"Perfect timing." He shakes his head with a chuckle as he takes Maisie's jacket for her and hangs it. Then he turns his attention to lighting the log in the fireplace.

Cat slinks around her ankles. "I brought you cookies," she says lightly, tossing him a smirk.

Dawson grumbles something under his breath, but I catch the way his lips twitch like he's fighting a smile. I pull Maisie into a hug. Then we settle into the living room, our chatter filling the space as Dawson gets to work stoking the fire.

An hour later the warmth wraps around us, cozy and familiar. A quiet kind of joy settles in my chest as I think about the way our lives will change a year from now. Emotion clogs my throat when I think of the life Dawson has built for us.

Boom. Boom. Boom.

Cat lets out an ear-splitting yowl at the sound of another knock on the front door. There's only one person it could be and we all know it. I look at Maisie and she gives me a faint nod that makes me bite back a smile. Dawson's jaw ticks and he looks from Maisie to me.

I hold up my hands. "I didn't know."

Maisie chews her bottom lip. "You two are going to love each other soon enough. He won't be here long, but I might have mentioned that he should stop by."

"Damn ranchers." Dawson mumbles as he pulls open the front door. "Kingridge, I didn't know you'd be joining us tonight."

Dear Reader,

Want more Dawson and Rosalie? *Subscribe to my newsletter, and I'll send you a bonus scene that takes place four years in the future! Get a glimpse of how Dawson is adjusting to life on the ranch… and how Rosalie is keeping him on his toes.*

Xoxo,

Elsie James

PS… Curious about Maisie's story, the podcast, and those rowdy ranchers? You can find them all in the Kingridge Ranch series!

ABOUT THE AUTHOR

I'm Elsie & I'm so happy you're here, you're going to fall in love tonight💕

I write short & steamy small-town romance stories about mountain men, lumberjacks, and ranchers. If you are looking to escape reality and fall into the arms of a man who will never let you down, you've come to the right place.

All of my books come with the promise of relatable characters, funny dialogue, no cheating, no cliffhangers & a happily ever after 💋

You deserve to treat yourself to falling in love with your new book boyfriend!

Hugs,

Elsie James

💋 ***Subscribe to my Newsletter and get a FREE EBook sent straight to your inbox!***

💋 Access exclusive deals when you shop directly with Elsie!

💋 Grab more delicious Bonus Content when you join the Treat Team as a FREE member on Patreon!

- Learn more: https://elsiejamesauthor.com/

www.ingramcontent.com/pod-product-compliance
Lightning Source LLC
Jackson TN
JSHW022229130425
82458JS00001B/52
9798230168898